D1712615

The route to your roots

When they look back at their formative years, many Indians nostalgically recall the vital part Amar Chitra Katha picture books have played in their lives. It was **ACK – Amar Chitra Katha** – that first gave them a glimpse of their glorious heritage.

Since they were introduced in 1967, there are now **over 400 Amar Chitra Katha** titles to choose from. **Over 90 million copies** have been sold worldwide.

Now the Amar Chitra Katha titles are even more widely available in **1000+ bookstores all across India**. Log on to www.ack-media.com to locate a bookstore near you. If you do not have access to a bookstore, you can buy all the titles through our online store **www.amar-chitrakatha.com**. We provide quick delivery anywhere in the world.

To make it easy for you to locate the titles of your choice from our treasure trove of titles, the books are now arranged in five categories.

Epics and Mythology
Best known stories from the Epics and the Puranas

Indian Classics
Enchanting tales from Indian literature

Fables and Humour
Evergreen folktales, legends and tales of wisdom and humour

Bravehearts
Stirring tales of brave men and women of India

Visionaries
Inspiring tales of thinkers, social reformers and nation builders

Contemporary Classics
The Best of Modern Indian literature

Amar Chitra Katha Pvt Ltd

© Amar Chitra Katha Pvt Ltd, 2010, Reprinted July 2013, ISBN 978-81-8482-399-8
Published & Printed by Amar Chitra Katha Pvt. Ltd., Krishna House, 3rd Floor,
Raghuvanshi Mill Compound, S.B.Marg, Lower Parel (W), Mumbai- 400 013. India
For Consumer Complaints Contact Tel : +91-22 40497436
Email: customerservice@ack-media.com

The route to your roots

ANDHER NAGARI

A disciple walks into a town where sweets and vegetable cost the same amount of money. Thrilled at being able to eat sweets so cheaply, he decides to stay there, ignoring his guru's warnings.

Bharatendu Harishchandra is one of the greatest playwrights in Hindi, and Andher Nagari, written in 1881, is his masterpiece.

Harishchandra's vision of a kingdom so ill-run that it is effectively blind to injustice remains a powerful image even today and the phrase 'andher nagari chaupat raja' (in the city of darkness, the king is insane) has passed into popular usage.

Script
Meera Ugra,
Luis Fernandes &
Sudha Nileshwar

Illustrations
Arvind Mandrekar

Editor
Anant Pai

ANY FRUIT! EVERY FRUIT! THE RATE IS THE SAME! TAKA SER! TAKA SER!

THIS IS INCREDIBLE! EVERYTHING HERE IS BEING SOLD FOR A TAKA A SER. WHAT A STRANGE PLACE!

TELL ME BROTHER, WHAT IS THE NAME OF YOUR TOWN? AND WHO IS THE RULER?

OUR TOWN IS CALLED ANDHER NAGARI. AND OUR KING'S NAME IS CHAUPAT RAJA.

ANDHER NAGARI, CHAUPAT RAJA! TAKA SER BHAJI,* TAKA SER KHAJA!+ THERE! I'VE COMPOSED A RHYME!

SO YOU HAVE. NOW WHAT WOULD YOU LIKE TO BUY, SIR?

SWEETS, OF COURSE! ONLY A FOOL WOULD BUY ANYTHING ELSE!

ANDHER NAGARI, CHAUPAT RAJA, TAKA SER BHAJI, TAKA SER KHAJA. ONLY A FOOL WOULD LEAVE THIS TOWN! SO THE GURU CERTAINLY WON'T!

*VEGETABLES   +A VARIETY OF SWEET

NARAYANDAS, DO YOU, TOO, WISH TO STAY?

NO, GURUJI.

THEN LET US GO.

HE IS A GREAT MAN, NO DOUBT, BUT A SIMPLETON WHEN IT COMES TO PRACTICAL MATTERS.

AHA! ANDHER NAGARI IS GREAT! LONG LIVE CHAUPAT RAJA— THE WISEST AND THE FAIREST OF KINGS!

GOVARDHANDAS PERHAPS WOULD NOT HAVE BEEN SO LAVISH IN HIS PRAISE OF THE KING IF HE COULD HAVE SEEN WHAT WAS HAPPENING AT THE PALACE AT THAT MOMENT.

JUSTICE! I WANT JUSTICE!

JUSTICE? DID SOMEONE ASK FOR JUSTICE? BRING HIM IN AT ONCE!

WHEN THE MAN WAS BROUGHT IN—

I WANT JUSTICE, MAHARAJ!

AND YOU SHALL HAVE IT. WHO HAS WRONGED YOU?

KALLU, THE GROCER, MAHARAJ. HIS WALL COLLAPSED AND MY GOAT··· MY POOR, INNOCENT GOAT··· WAS CRUSHED UNDER IT!

THE KING TURNED TO HIS MINISTER.

SUMMON KALLU'S WALL TO THE COURT! AT ONCE!

BUT MAHARAJ, THE WALL CAN'T BE BROUGHT HERE!

WHAT A PITY! NEVER MIND. CALL THE WALL'S NEXT OF KIN THEN.

A BRICK AND LIME WALL DOESN'T HAVE NEXT OF KIN, MAHARAJ.

JUSTICE, MAHARAJ!

ALL RIGHT, ALL RIGHT! BRING KALLU HERE, IMMEDIATELY!

YES, MAHARAJ.

THE GROCER WAS BROUGHT TO THE PALACE.

YOUR NEIGHBOUR SAYS YOUR WALL COLLAPSED ON HIS GOAT.

WHAT DO YOU HAVE TO SAY FOR YOURSELF?

IT...IT WAS NOT M-MY FAULT, MAHARAJ.

IF... IF THE CONTRACTOR HAD BUILT A STRONGER WALL IT WOULD NEVER HAVE COLLAPSED.

THE CONTRACTOR WAS BROUGHT BEFORE THE KING.

THE WALL YOU BUILT COLLAPSED AND A GOAT WAS KILLED!

DO YOU HAVE ANYTHING TO SAY IN YOUR DEFENCE?

YOU HAVE GOT THE WRONG MAN, MAHARAJ! IT'S THE WATER-CARRIER WHO IS TO BE BLAMED.

BECAUSE HE POURED TOO MUCH WATER ON THE LIME, THE BRICKS WERE NOT FIRMLY JOINED. THAT'S WHY THE WALL COLLAPSED!

WHEN THE WATER-CARRIER WAS SUMMONED—

IT WAS THE COBBLER'S FAULT, MAHARAJ. HE MADE MY WATER-BAG EXTRA LARGE.

WHEN THE COBBLER WAS BROUGHT IN—

I AM INNOCENT, MAHARAJ. THE BUTCHER SOLD ME THAT HUGE SHEEPSKIN.

THE BUTCHER TOO HAD A READY EXPLANATION.

A THOUSAND APOLOGIES, MAHARAJ. BUT OUR KOTWAL* PASSED BY IN SUCH A GRAND PROCESSION THAT MY ATTENTION WAS DIVERTED AND I SUPPLIED TOO LARGE A SHEEPSKIN BY MISTAKE.

GET THE KOTWAL HERE! IMMEDIATELY!

SOON THE KOTWAL TOO WAS QUESTIONED.

IT WASN'T A GRAND PROCESSION, MAHARAJ. I WAS JUST DOING MY ROUNDS OF THE CITY.

*POLICE CHIEF

BUT WHY SUCH POMP AND SHOW THAT THE BUTCHER'S ATTENTION WAS DIVERTED?

YES. WHY? ANSWER THAT!

BUT... BUT... YOUR MAJESTY...

NO BUTS... I'VE HAD ENOUGH OF THIS.

TAKE THE KOTWAL AWAY AND HANG HIM! THE COURT IS DISMISSED!

MERCY, MAHARAJ! PLEASE HAVE PITY ON ME!

JUSTICE KNOWS NO MERCY! TAKE HIM AWAY.

THE UNFORTUNATE KOTWAL WAS LED TO THE GALLOWS.

LET ME GO! PLEASE LET ME GO!

PUT THE NOOSE ROUND HIS NECK!

THE MINISTER WAS SOON BACK WITH THE KING'S ORDERS.

GO AND FIND A FAT MAN. AND BE QUICK ABOUT IT.

AND MAKE SURE HE HAS A THICK NECK.

THE SOLDIERS LOOKED EVERYWHERE FOR A FAT MAN...

...BUT ALL THE FAT MEN HAD GONE INTO HIDING.

13

LOOK, BROTHERS, I AM A MAN OF GOD AND I AM NOT FAMILIAR WITH THE WAYS OF THE WORLD.

YOU'LL SOON BE DEPARTING FROM IT, SO IT DOESN'T MATTER.

I? DEPARTING FROM THE WORLD? SURELY THERE'S SOME MISTAKE.

HANGMAN? DEPARTING FROM THE WORLD?

Y-YOU MEAN I-I AM GOING TO BE... BE...

EXACTLY.

BUT WHY?

BECAUSE YOU ARE FAT.

BECAUSE I AM FAT?

DON'T GET UPSET.

SEE THE BRIGHT SIDE OF THINGS. EVERY MAN WHO IS TO BE HANGED IS GRANTED A LAST WISH. SEE HOW LUCKY YOU ARE!

AH! HERE WE ARE! YOU CAN ASK FOR ANYTHING YOU WANT... ANYTHING! JUST IMAGINE!

WHAT TOOK YOU SO LONG? DID YOU HAVE TO FEED HIM TO FATTEN HIM?

GET HIM UP THERE QUICKLY!

YES, SIR.

AS GOVARDHANDAS WAS LED UP TO THE GALLOWS—

LISTEN, BROTHERS! PLEASE SPARE ME, I AM AN INNOCENT MAN! I WOULDN'T HURT A FLY! I...

MAY I HAVE A FEW WORDS WITH MY DISCIPLE IN PRIVATE? MY LAST SERMON TO HIM. YOU HAVE NO OBJECTION, I HOPE.

NONE, WHATSOEVER, HOLY ONE. PLEASE GO AHEAD.

I CAN'T BELIEVE IT! HOW ABSOLUTELY DIVINE! OH, HOW FORTUNATE I AM!

I CAN'T WAIT ANYMORE! PLEASE HANG ME SOON! THIS MOMENT!

NO, WAIT!

?

YOU CAN'T DO THIS TO ME, YOUR GURU. I MUST BE HANGED IN YOUR PLACE. PLEASE!

BUT YOU CAN'T DEPRIVE ME OF MY GOOD LUCK, GURUJI.

SON, I AM AN OLD MAN. YOU SHOULD CONCEDE THIS PRIVILEGE TO ME.

YOU FORGET IT WAS I WHO WAS SENTENCED.

BESIDES, YOU ARE A SAINT. YOU'LL GO TO HEAVEN IN ANY CASE, WHEREAS THIS IS MY ONLY CHANCE.

JUST THEN—

WHAT'S GOING ON HERE? WHY HAVEN'T YOU HANGED THIS MAN AS YET?

IT'S QUITE PUZZLING, MAHARAJ. BOTH, THIS MAN AND HIS GURU, ARE EQUALLY KEEN ON BEING HANGED.

MAHARAJ, I DESERVE TO BE HANGED. I WAS THE CHOSEN ONE.

DON'T LISTEN TO MY DISCIPLE, MAHARAJ. PLEASE HANG ME!

BUT WHY, O HOLY ONE? WHY DO YOU WANT TO DIE?

BECAUSE I KNOW WHAT NOBODY... NOBODY EXCEPT MY DISCIPLE... KNOWS.

AND WHAT IS IT?

WELL... YOUR MAJESTY... I HAVE DIVINED THAT WHOEVER DIES AT THIS MOMENT WILL GO STRAIGHT TO HEAVEN!

REALLY? THEN I SHOULD BE THE ONE TO BE HANGED.

NO, NO, NO! REMEMBER THE WALL FELL BECAUSE OF ME.

BUT I AM THE FAT ONE.

BE QUIET, ALL OF YOU! HOW DARE ANYONE TALK OF GOING TO HEAVEN WHEN I, THE SOVEREIGN, AM HERE! IT IS MY BIRTHRIGHT TO GO TO HEAVEN!

HANG ME! HANG ME, THIS MOMENT! I COMMAND YOU!

DON'T FEEL SORRY FOR HIM, MY CHILDREN. HE INVITED IT UPON HIMSELF.

HAZAAR MAARYA

IN THE KINGDOM OF RAJPUR THERE LIVED A LAZY MAN CALLED BALU.

HIS WIFE SONUBAI WAS ALWAYS TRYING TO GET HIM TO DO SOME WORK.

HEY!

GO AND CHOP SOME WOOD FOR THE FIRE.

A MAN CAN'T SLEEP IN PEACE AROUND HERE... OH! THESE FLIES!

HEY! I'VE KILLED SEVEN OF THEM! WHAT AN ACHIEVEMENT!

I WONDER HOW MANY I COULD FINISH OFF IN A WHOLE DAY.

AT LAST ONE DAY—

HA! THAT MAKES THE THOUSANDTH FLY! I'VE KILLED A THOUSAND.

HE HAS KILLED A THOUSAND!

THERE GOES THE KILLER OF A THOUSAND!

AND SO THE WORD SPREAD IN THE TOWN...

...AND THROUGHOUT THE KINGDOM OF RAJPUR.

THAT MAN IS A KILLER OF A THOUSAND.

AHA! HAZAAR MAARYA!

SOME DAYS LATER AT THE KING'S COURT—

MAHARAJ, OUR ENEMIES ARE AT THE CITY GATES.

THERE ARE THOUSANDS OF SOLDIERS, SEVERAL HUNDRED HORSES AND AT LEAST A HUNDRED ELEPHANTS.

THEIR SWORDS AND ARMOUR DAZZLE THE EYE.

23

OUR ARMY IS STRONG ENOUGH, MAHARAJ. BUT WE LACK AN ABLE GENERAL.

SEND OUT A DOZEN MESSENGERS TO LOOK FOR A WORTHY MAN. HE SHOULD BE HERE BEFORE SUNDOWN.

THE SEARCH BEGAN. MESSENGERS WERE DESPATCHED TO EVERY CORNER OF THE KINGDOM.

ONE MESSENGER RODE TO THE MARKET-PLACE. THERE—

HERE COMES HAZAAR MAARYA!

HE'S THE GREAT WARRIOR WHO HAS KILLED A THOUSAND, ISN'T HE?

THE MESSENGER RUSHED BACK TO THE KING.

MAHARAJ, THE PEOPLE OF THE CITY SPEAK HIGHLY OF A BRAVE WARRIOR KNOWN AS HAZAAR MAARYA!

SUMMON HIM HERE!

VERY SOON, AT HAZAAR MAARYA'S COTTAGE—

O BRAVE WARRIOR, THE KING WISHES TO HONOUR YOU WITH A HIGH OFFICE.

A HIGH OFFICE?

PLEASE COME WITH ME TO THE PALACE.

CERTAINLY!

I MUST BE DREAMING!

LATER, AT THE PALACE—

SO YOU ARE THE FAMOUS HAZAAR MAARYA. WE ARE TOLD YOU HAVE KILLED A THOUSAND.

THAT'S TRUE, MAHARAJ.

I GIVE YOU THE COMMAND OF ALL MY ARMIES, AND ORDER YOU TO LEAD THEM TO VICTORY AGAINST OUR ENEMIES.

I SHALL DO MY BEST TO OBEY YOUR COMMANDS AND BRING GLORY TO YOU, MAHARAJ.

YOUR HORSE AND ARMOUR SHALL BE SENT TO YOUR COTTAGE.

YOUR WISH IS MY COMMAND, YOUR MAJESTY.

THAT NIGHT AT THE ENEMY CAMP—

DO YOU KNOW WHO IS TO LEAD THE ARMY OF RAJPUR TOMORROW?

IT'S HAZAAR MAARYA!

HAZAAR MAARYA... THE KILLER OF A THOUSAND.

THE NEWS SPREAD LIKE WILDFIRE THROUGHOUT THE ENEMY CAMP.

WHEN MORNING DAWNED —

I SHALL BRING VICTORY AND HONOUR TO RAJPUR TODAY.

INDEED YOU SHALL, MY LORD!

BUT I'D BETTER NOT TAKE ANY CHANCES. THE COWARD MIGHT JUMP OFF HIS HORSE AND RUN AWAY DURING THE BATTLE.

WHAT ARE YOU DOING?

I AM TYING YOU TO YOUR HORSE, MY LORD.

OTHERWISE IN YOUR EAGERNESS TO FIGHT YOU MIGHT JUMP OFF THE HORSE AND ATTACK THE ENEMY ON FOOT.

LATER AT THE PALACE GROUNDS —

WELCOME, BRAVE GENERAL! THIS IS YOUR ARMY. NOW LEAD IT TO VICTORY!

I SHALL DO MY BEST, MAHARAJ.

26

THE ARMY RODE OUT...

...TO THE BATTLEFIELD.

WHAT A HUGE ARMY THEY HAVE!

MY GOD, THEY ARE SHOOTING AT US! I... I COULD VERY EASILY GET HURT HERE!

WHAT SHOULD WE DO, SIR?

RETREAT! I MEAN ATTACK! BUT LET'S NOT GO TOO CLOSE!

THE RAJPUR ARMY WAS SOON ROUTED.

MY SOLDIERS ARE RUNNING AWAY. I MUST SAVE MYSELF.

OH, THAT WIFE OF MINE! WHY DID SHE HAVE TO TIE ME UP SO TIGHTLY!

AS HAZAAR MAARYA STRUGGLED TO FREE HIMSELF, HIS HORSE SUDDENLY PANICKED...

...AND BEGAN TO RUN TOWARDS THE ENEMY CAMP.

STOP! YOU STUPID BEAST! STOP!

OH, I'M DONE FOR!

HELP! HELP!

THERE WAS A CLUMP OF BAMBOO BETWEEN THE RAJPUR ARMY AND THE ENEMY LINES AND THE HORSE RODE STRAIGHT TOWARDS IT.

HAZAAR MAARYA CLUTCHED AT THE BAMBOO TREES TO SAVE HIMSELF...

...BUT THE STALKS WERE ROTTEN AT THE ROOTS AND CAME OFF IN HIS HANDS.

NOW MY END IS NEAR!

THE ENEMY SOLDIERS HOWEVER, WERE UNAWARE OF WHAT WAS REALLY HAPPENING. THEY THOUGHT HAZAAR MAARYA WAS COMING TO ATTACK THEM.

THAT MAN HAS NO FEAR!

SEE HOW FEROCIOUSLY HE'S WAVING THOSE BAMBOOS!

WHAT SHOULD WE DO?

RUN!

HE HAS BEEN KNOWN TO KILL A THOUSAND MEN SINGLE-HANDED!

THUS THE LAZY BALU BECAME THE BRAVE GENERAL, HAZAAR MAARYA, FAMOUS FOR HIS RARE COURAGE; AND FROM THAT DAY HE DIDN'T KILL A SINGLE FLY!

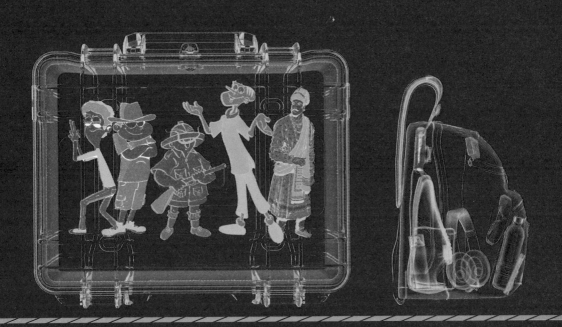

MANDUKA

THE ACCIDENTAL ASTROLOGER

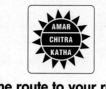

The route to your roots

MANDUKA

Named after a frog, Manduka has spent his entire life being scorned by everyone around him. So he decides to pretend to be a wise astrologer, and get people to respect him. His plan works beyond his wildest dreams.

Now Manduka finds himself in a different kind of fix: people are actually expecting him to make accurate predictions. Worse, the king himself is asking for Manduka's prophecies!

The story of Manduka is taken from the Kathasaritsagar, the eleventh century Sanskrit classic by Somadeva.

Script
Luis M. Fernandes

Illustrations
Ram Waeerkar

Editor
Anant Pai

MANDUKA- THE LUCKY ASTROLOGER

ONE DAY A POOR BRAHMANA WAS PASSING BY THE HOUSE OF A MERCHANT.

HEY! THERE'S A WEDDING GOING ON THERE!

NO ONE EVEN BOTHERED TO TELL ME ABOUT IT.

WHO TELLS ME ANYTHING? EVEN WHEN I WAS A CHILD, EVERYBODY IGNORED ME.

EXCEPT FATHER, OF COURSE, WHO NEVER FAILED TO TELL ME ONE THING EVERY SO OFTEN.

YOU ARE AS DULL AS A MANDUKA* IN A WELL.

1

THAT'S WHAT I'VE BECOME, A MANDUKA! AND I'M TIRED OF IT.

?!

I WISH I COULD DO SOMETHING... ANYTHING... WHICH WOULD MAKE EVERYONE...

...SIT UP AND TAKE NOTICE OF ME.

HEY, I'VE GOT IT!

THE BRAHMANA RAN BACK...

...TO THE PLACE WHERE THE WEDDING WAS GOING ON...

...AND QUIETLY LED AWAY THE HORSE ON WHICH THE BRIDEGROOM HAD COME.

THE NEXT MORNING—

MASTER, THE BRIDEGROOM'S HORSE HAS DISAPPEARED!

DISAPPEARED?

HOW COULD IT DISAPPEAR? GO AND LOOK FOR IT!

WE ALREADY HAVE, MASTER.

IT HAS VANISHED WITHOUT A TRACE.

OH, THIS IS TERRIBLE!

WHAT AM I TO DO NOW?

MASTER, THERE'S A WOMAN OUTSIDE WHO SAYS WE SHOULD SEEK THE HELP OF HER HUSBAND.

SHE SAYS HE'S AN ASTROLOGER.

GO FETCH HIM AT ONCE!

SOMETIME LATER—

THE ASTROLOGER IS HERE, MASTER.

3

COME IN, COME IN, SIR.

HOW WELL MY PLAN IS WORKING! ALREADY I'M BEING TREATED AS AN HONOURED GUEST.

YOUR SERVANTS TELL ME YOU HAVE LOST A HORSE.

THAT'S RIGHT.

I SHALL REWARD YOU HANDSOMELY IF YOU CAN HELP US FIND HIM.

GIVE ME A FEW MOMENTS AND I SHALL TELL YOU EXACTLY WHERE HE IS.

I'LL HAVE TO STUDY THESE CHARTS AND... AND... AH!

YOU'LL FIND THE HORSE NEAR THE STREAM. BUT MAKE HASTE, HE IS IN DANGER OF BEING STOLEN.

RUSH TO THE STREAM!

4

SOON PEOPLE EVERYWHERE BEGAN TO SHOW HIM RESPECT.

EVERYONE BOWS TO ME NOW.

AT LAST THE MANDUKA HAS JUMPED OUT OF THE WELL!

?!

HE TALKS TO HIMSELF!

ALL GREAT MEN HAVE SOME PECULIARITY OR OTHER.

THE BRAHMANA'S FAME SPREAD FAR AND WIDE. THEN ONE DAY—

ARE YOU PANDIT BHOJRAJ?

YES.

YOUR PRESENCE IS REQUESTED AT THE PALACE. PLEASE COME WITH ME.

LATER, AT THE PALACE—

THE QUEEN'S NECKLACE HAS BEEN LOST...OR STOLEN....

I HAVE HEARD THAT YOU ONCE TOLD A MERCHANT WHERE HE COULD FIND HIS LOST HORSE.

I AM SURE YOU CAN TELL US WHERE THE NECKLACE IS.

I.... ER....

NOW WHAT AM I TO DO?

WELL?

I.... I NEED TIME.

YOU CAN TAKE AS LONG AS YOU WANT.

BUT YOU MUST NOT LEAVE THE PALACE TILL THE NECKLACE IS FOUND.

THIS IS THE END OF THE ROAD FOR ME.

I WONDER WHAT THE KING WILL DO TO ME WHEN HE DISCOVERS THAT I AM NOT A REAL ASTROLOGER.

7

THE BRAHMANA SHUT HIMSELF UP IN HIS CHAMBER AND PREPARED FOR THE WORST.

WELL...WHY DID I CLAIM TO BE WHAT I AM NOT? NOW I WILL JUST HAVE TO PAY FOR IT.

IT'S MY TONGUE WHICH HAS GOT ME INTO ALL THIS TROUBLE.

JUST THEN, OUTSIDE THE CHAMBER—

HE IS A GREAT ASTROLOGER.

HE WILL SOON KNOW THAT IT IS I WHO STOLE THE NECKLACE.

WHY, OH, WHY DID I DO SUCH A FOOLISH THING!

LET ME SEE WHAT HE IS DOING.

THE BRAHMANA, UNAWARE THAT THE MAID WAS PEEPING THROUGH THE KEYHOLE, BEGAN TO SCOLD HIS TONGUE.

WHAT HAVE YOU DONE, JIHVAH*? WHY DID YOU DO IT?

*TONGUE (SANSKRIT)

HE KNOWS!

I AM DOOMED!

O HOLY SIR, HAVE MERCY ON ME!

I DID IT IN A MOMENT OF WEAKNESS.

DID WHAT? WHO ARE YOU?

I AM JIHVAH, THE MAID. I HEARD YOU.

I...I DON'T KNOW WHY I STOLE THE NECKLACE.

SHE THOUGHT I WAS TALKING TO HER.

PLEASE DON'T TELL THE KING!

ER... WELL...

YOU HAVE COMMITTED A GREAT SIN. BUT I SHALL FORGIVE YOU THIS ONCE. NOW WHERE IS THE NECKLACE?

LATER THAT DAY, AS THE KING WAS STROLLING IN THE GARDEN—

I KNOW WHERE THE NECKLACE IS, MAHARAJ. PLEASE FOLLOW ME.

?

HERE.

A GARDENER BEGAN TO DIG UP THE EARTH.

SOON—

THE NECKLACE!

YOU ARE WITHOUT DOUBT THE GREATEST ASTROLOGER I HAVE EVER MET!

NOW TELL ME WHO HID THE NECKLACE HERE?

THAT MUST REMAIN A SECRET, MAHARAJ.

THERE ARE SOME THINGS WHICH EVEN I MAY NOT KNOW.

THERE IS SOME MYSTERY HERE, MAHARAJ. IF HE IS SUCH A GREAT ASTROLOGER WHY CAN'T HE TELL US WHO THE THIEF IS?

HE MUST HAVE FOUND THE NECKLACE IN THE PALACE AND HIDDEN IT HERE HIMSELF.

DO YOU THINK SO?

LET US TEST HIM ONCE MORE.

ALL RIGHT.

I AM AMAZED BY YOUR POWER, O PANDIT, AND YOU SHALL BE WELL REWARDED FOR YOUR SERVICES.

BUT DO NOT LEAVE THE PALACE AS YET.

I.... I WONDER WHAT HE HAS IN MIND.

AFTER SOME TIME, THE BRAHMANA WAS SUMMONED TO THE KING'S CHAMBER.

COME IN, PANDITJI.

CAN YOU TELL US WHAT IS IN THAT JAR?

HOW NEATLY HE HAS TRAPPED ME!

NOW I'LL HAVE TO TELL HIM THAT I AM NOT REALLY AN ASTROLOGER...

...AND THAT I FOOLED HIM AND EVERYBODY ELSE.

HE'LL SURELY PUT ME TO DEATH!

O MANDUKA,* YOU WERE BETTER OFF IN THE WELL.

WELL DONE! I SHOULD NEVER HAVE DOUBTED YOUR POWERS.

EH!

THERE IS INDEED A MANDUKA IN THE JAR.

THE KING REWARDED THE BRAHMANA WITH COSTLY GIFTS...

...AND HE RETURNED HOME TO A HERO'S WELCOME.

*FROG

12

THE HIDDEN MEANING

THERE WAS ONCE A FARMER. HE WAS HARD-WORKING BUT NOT TOO BRIGHT AND EVERYONE CALLED HIM BUDDHURAM. HE WAS A CONTENTED SOUL AND HAD NO AMBITIONS.

HIS WIFE HOWEVER WAS EXACTLY THE OPPOSITE.

OUR NEIGHBOUR'S SON-IN-LAW HAS BOUGHT TWO BUFFALOES!

EVERYONE IS BUYING BUFFALOES OR LAND··· EXCEPT US.

YOU MUST MAKE MONEY SOMEHOW.

DID YOU HEAR ME?

YES, YES!

13

NOW PLEASE LET ME EAT IN PEACE!

HMMPH!

SOMETIMES I FEEL LIKE BREAKING A POT OVER HIS THICK SKULL!

MATTERS CAME TO A HEAD WHEN ONE DAY THE NEIGHBOUR EXCITEDLY BURST INTO THE HOUSE.

YOU WON'T BELIEVE IT!

WHAT?

MY HUSBAND HAS BEEN HONOURED BY THE KING!

WHAT!

ARE YOU ALL RIGHT?

YES, YES! DON'T WORRY ABOUT ME··· IT'S THE HEAT!

OH, WHAT MARVELLOUS NEWS···ER, FOR WHAT DID THE KING HONOUR HIM?

FOR HIS POETRY.

POETRY?

YES. HE RECITED ONE OF HIS POEMS TO THE KING.

THE KING WAS SO PLEASED WITH IT THAT HE PRESENTED MY HUSBAND WITH TWO GOLD COINS!

TWO GOLD COINS!

HOW MARVELLOUS!

ISN'T IT? IF YOU'LL EXCUSE ME, I MUST RUSH HOME.

FROM NOW ON I WON'T HAVE A MOMENT'S REST. EVERYONE WILL WANT TO MEET MY HUSBAND!

AND FROM NOW ON SHE'LL BECOME EVEN MORE INSUFFERABLE.

IT'S ALL BECAUSE OF THAT DIM-WITTED HUSBAND OF MINE! IF ONLY HE WOULD DO SOMETHING SPECTACULAR!

THERE HE COMES!

HAVE YOU HEARD THE NEWS?

WHAT NEWS?

OUR GOOD NEIGHBOUR HAS BEEN HONOURED BY THE KING!

THE KING GAVE HIM TWO GOLD COINS FOR A POEM HE HAD WRITTEN!

IMAGINE! TWO GOLD COINS!

WHAT VEGETABLE HAVE YOU COOKED TODAY?

THACK

PEOPLE AROUND US HAVE BECOME RICH AND FAMOUS AND...

THE FIRST LETTER OF THE ALPHABET IS 'A'.

OH!

NOT 'O' 'A'

IT'S WRITTEN LIKE··· THIS!

NOW GO TO THE RIVERSIDE AND PRACTISE WRITING IT IN THE SAND!

EVERY DAY HIS WIFE WOULD TEACH HIM ONE LETTER OF THE ALPHABET···

···AND THEN SHE WOULD SEND HIM TO THE RIVERSIDE TO PRACTISE WRITING IT.

* THE FIRST LETTER OF THE SANSKRIT ALPHABET

BUT POOR BUDDHURAM HAD A BAD MEMORY.

NOW WHAT DID SHE SAY THE THIRD LETTER WAS?

EEEE? BEEE? EHH?

WHAT ARE YOU DOING MY GOOD MAN?

I AM... ER LEARNING THE ALPHABET SO THAT I CAN WRITE POETRY.

YOU WANT TO WRITE POETRY, DO YOU?

AND DO YOU THINK EVERYONE WHO KNOWS THE ALPHABET CAN WRITE POETRY?

YOU NEED INSPIRATION TO WRITE POETRY, MY FRIEND! INSPIRATION!

WHO'S THAT?

NOT WHO, WHAT. INSPIRATION IS A FEELING! WHEN YOU GET INSPIRED A THRILL RUNS THROUGH YOUR BODY AND··· AND···

···OH! NEVER MIND!

I HOPE MY WIFE DOESN'T KNOW ABOUT INSPIRATION OR SHE'LL MAKE ME STUDY THAT TOO.

WHEN HE RETURNED HOME HE HAD TO RECITE ALL THE LETTERS HIS WIFE HAD TAUGHT HIM.

I···UH···HAVE FORGOTTEN THE THIRD LETTER···

THEN YOU DON'T GET ANY FOOD!

SLAM

LIFE BECAME MISERABLE FOR BUDDHURAM.

WHY DOESN'T SHE LEAVE ME ALONE? I WAS HAPPY JUST BEING A FARMER.

WHAT A STROKE OF LUCK! BUT NOW THAT I HAVE GOT INSPIRATION I MUST WRITE A POEM!

BUT ABOUT WHAT? ABOUT WHOM?

AH, THAT CROW····! HE IS SHARPENING HIS BEAK IN EXPECTATION OF A FEAST.

YOU DIP IT IN WATER AND SHARPEN IT··· AGAIN AND AGAIN.

O, KALIA I CAN READ YOUR MIND!

22

THERE! I HAVE COMPOSED A POEM!

YOU DIP IT IN WATER AND SHARPEN IT, AGAIN AND AGAIN. O KALIA, I CAN READ YOUR MIND.

?

OH, WHAT A POEM! MY WIFE WILL BE ASTOUNDED!

BUDDHURAM RAN HOME.

WIFE! WIFE! I HAVE COMPOSED A POEM!

YES! I ENTERED THE RIVER AND SUDDENLY I HAD...

...INSPIRATION! SEIZING THE OPPORTUNITY, I IMMEDIATELY COMPOSED A POEM. LISTEN...

23

YOU DIP IT IN WATER AND SHARPEN IT AGAIN AND AGAIN. O KALIA, I CAN READ YOUR MIND.

WHAT DO YOU THINK OF IT?

I...ER... IS THAT A POEM?

OF COURSE, IT IS! I HAD INSPIRATION I TELL YOU!

PERHAPS IT IS A POEM. WHO CAN TELL? PERHAPS THE GODDESS HAD PITY ON MY POOR HUSBAND AND ON ME AND INSPIRED HIM THE WAY SHE INSPIRED KALIDASA.

WELL, NOW THAT YOU HAVE A POEM, YOU'D BETTER GO TO THE PALACE AND RECITE IT BEFORE THE KING.

SO BUDDHURAM SET OFF FOR THE PALACE.

YOU DIP IT IN WATER, AND SHARPEN IT...

24

WHEN HE GOT THERE—

I HAVE COME TO RECITE A POEM.

YOU CAN GO IN. THE SESSION HAS JUST BEGUN.

BUDDHURAM WENT IN AND TOOK HIS PLACE AMONG THE POETS.

SOME OF THESE MEN WERE FAMED THROUGHOUT THE LAND AND THEY HELD THE AUDIENCE SPELLBOUND.

BUDDHURAM WAITED IMPATIENTLY FOR HIS TURN. FINALLY THE LAST MAN FINISHED HIS RECITATION.

NOW THEY'LL KNOW WHAT REAL POETRY IS.

IS THERE ANYBODY LEFT?

YES!!!

YOU MAY BEGIN, THEN.

BUDDHURAM CLEARED HIS THROAT, THREW OUT HIS CHEST AND BEGAN TO RECITE HIS COMPOSITION IN A LOUD BOOMING VOICE.

YOU DIP IT IN WATER AND SHARPEN IT AGAIN AND AGAIN. O KALIA, I CAN READ YOUR MIND.

IS THAT A POEM?

?

THE WHOLE AUDIENCE BURST OUT LAUGHING...

HAHAHAHOH HOHOHOHOH KHIKHI HIHIHI

...BUT THE KING MAINTAINED A DISCREET SILENCE.

NO ONE WOULD DARE TO COME HERE AND RECITE SUCH NONSENSE UNLESS THERE WAS SOME MEANING IN THE WORDS.

AND THE MAN APPEARS SO CONFIDENT. HE'S SURELY NOT A FOOL.

HE TURNED TO HIS MINISTER.

WELL, WHAT DID YOU THINK OF THE POEM?

I... WELL...

HE DIDN'T LAUGH WITH THE REST OF US. PERHAPS THE WORDS HAVE SOME SIGNIFICANCE WHICH THE REST OF US MISSED.

IT IS OBVIOUS THAT THE POEM IS···ER··· PREGNANT WITH MEANING, MAHARAJ.

JUST AS I THOUGHT.

CAN YOU INTERPRET IT?

I··· UH···NO, MAHARAJ.

CAN ANYONE INTERPRET THE POEM?

INTERPRET? I THOUGHT IT WAS JUST NONSENSE.

!?

LET THE POEM BE WRITTEN ON A BOARD IN THE COURTYARD.

IF ANYONE CAN INTERPRET THE POEM, HE SHALL BE REWARDED WITH TEN GOLD COINS!

TEN GOLD COINS!

WHAT ABOUT ME, MAHARAJ?

YOU TOO WILL GET YOUR REWARD... BUT IN DUE COURSE.

BUDDHURAM'S COMPOSITION WAS WRITTEN ON A HUGE BOARD AND THE BOARD WAS SET UP IN THE COURTYARD.

YOU DIP IT IN WATER, AND SHARPEN IT, AGAIN AND AGAIN. O KALIA, I CAN READ YOUR MIND.

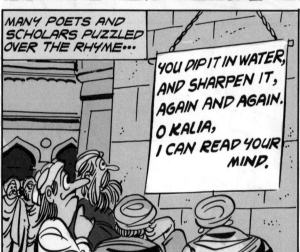

MANY POETS AND SCHOLARS PUZZLED OVER THE RHYME...

YOU DIP IT IN WATER, AND SHARPEN IT, AGAIN AND AGAIN. O KALIA, I CAN READ YOUR MIND.

...BUT NO ONE COULD SEE ANY SPECIAL MEANING IN THE WORDS.

DAYS PASSED. THEN ONE MORNING, AS THE KING WAS BEING PREPARED FOR A SHAVE BY HIS BARBER —

WHAT'S THE MATTER, KALIA? YOU SEEM RATHER NERVOUS TODAY?

I... I'M ALL RIGHT, MAHARAJ.

THE BARBER PICKED UP HIS RAZOR...

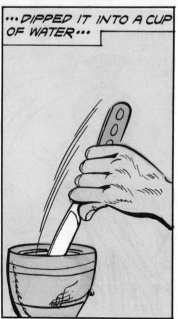

...DIPPED IT INTO A CUP OF WATER...

...AND BEGAN TO SHARPEN IT.

YOU DIP IT IN WATER AND SHARPEN IT...

?

...AGAIN AND AGAIN. O KALIA, I CAN READ YOUR MIND.

WHAT!

FORGIVE ME, MAHARAJ!

IT WAS NOT MY IDEA AT ALL! THEY ASKED ME TO DO IT!

DO WHAT?

CUT YOUR THROAT.

OH, I SEE IT ALL NOW.

THAT POEM WAS A PROPHECY AND ALSO A WARNING TO THE BARBER. I AM FORTUNATE I RECITED IT JUST NOW.

GUARD!

ARREST THIS MAN AND TAKE DOWN HIS STATEMENT.

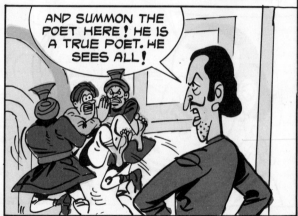

AND SUMMON THE POET HERE! HE IS A TRUE POET. HE SEES ALL!

SO IT WAS THAT BUDDHURAM BECAME A GREAT HERO. THE KING REWARDED HIM HANDSOMELY AND HE RETURNED HOME, RICH AND FAMOUS.

OH, WHAT A WONDERFUL MAN MY HUSBAND IS!

THE MIRACULOUS CONCH
AND A GAME OF CHESS

THE MIRACULOUS CONCH

A very poor man is given a magical conch – when it is put in a pot and food is cooked with it, the pot supplies an endless quantity of very delicious food. When the conch goes missing, the man and his companions, a dog and a cat, must find it before they starve.

A tyrannical king decrees that anyone who wants a favour from him, has to play chess with him. Sitting near by will be the king's cat, with seven lamps balanced on her tail. If she moves and even a drop of oil is spilt, the king will do as his opponent wants. But if the cat remains still, the person will become the king's slave!

The hilarious adventures in this book, are taken from John Dorairaj's collection of folk tales.

Script
Luis Fernandes

Illustrations
Ram Waeerkar

Editor
Anant Pai

THE MIRACULOUS CONCH

ONCE UPON A TIME THERE WAS A MAN WHO WAS POOR BUT GENEROUS. HIS ONLY COMPANIONS WERE A CAT AND A DOG.

OH, THERE'S SOMEONE AT THE DOOR.

I HAVE WALKED A LONG DISTANCE AND I AM WEARY.

COME IN. COME IN.

USE THE WATER IN THAT POT IF YOU WANT TO HAVE A WASH FIRST. I'LL GET YOU SOMETHING TO EAT.

THE MAN GAVE HIS GUEST ALL THE RICE HE HAD COOKED FOR HIS COMPANIONS AND HIM-SELF.

THE GUEST ATE UP EVERY GRAIN OF IT.

NOW IF I COULD LIE DOWN SOMEWHERE...

MAKE YOURSELF COMFORTABLE ON THIS COT, SIR.

THE CAT, THE DOG AND THEIR MASTER WENT HUNGRY THAT NIGHT.

EARLY NEXT MORNING —

I FEEL REFRESHED. I AM GRATEFUL TO YOU FOR YOUR HOSPITALITY.

BEFORE I GO, HERE IS SOMETHING FOR YOU.

DROP THAT CONCH INTO THE POT THE NEXT TIME YOU COOK RICE.

WHAT'S THE USE OF A CONCH?

NOW IF IT HAD BEEN MONEY, OUR MASTER COULD HAVE BOUGHT US SOME FOOD. I AM STARVING.

THAT AFTERNOON AS THE OLD MAN WAS COOKING A HANDFUL OF RICE WHICH HE HAD BORROWED FROM A NEIGHBOUR—

I'LL DROP THE CONCH IN AND SEE WHAT HAPPENS. IT MAY IMPROVE THE TASTE.

THE MOMENT HE DROPPED THE CONCH INTO THE POT...

...A DELICIOUS AROMA ROSE UP FROM IT.

MMM...MMM!

I WONDER WHAT THE OLD MAN IS COOKING!

LET'S FIND OUT!

WHAT ARE YOU COOKING, FRIEND?

RICE.

MAY WE HAVE SOME?

CERTAINLY. AS SOON AS IT'S DONE.

BUT THE APPETIZING AROMA KEPT ATTRACTING MORE AND MORE PEOPLE AND THE GENEROUS OLD MAN DID NOT HAVE THE HEART TO SEND ANY OF THEM AWAY.

SO WHEN THE RICE WAS READY THERE WERE A LOT OF PEOPLE WAITING TO EAT IT.

I'LL BE ABLE TO GIVE ONLY A FEW GRAINS TO EACH OF THEM.

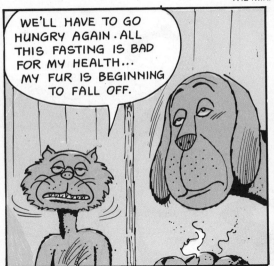

WE'LL HAVE TO GO HUNGRY AGAIN. ALL THIS FASTING IS BAD FOR MY HEALTH... MY FUR IS BEGINNING TO FALL OFF.

HERE YOU ARE, SIR.

AND A LITTLE FOR YOU.

WHEN THE OLD MAN HAD SERVED ALL OF THEM —

WHY, THERE'S STILL A LOT LEFT!

HAVE SOME MORE.

I COULD DO WITH A SECOND HELPING TOO. THIS RICE IS SIMPLY DELICIOUS!

THE OTHERS TOO ASKED FOR MORE. WHEN ALL OF THEM HAD BEEN SERVED —

WHAT! THE RICE IS NOT OVER YET!

6

EVERY TIME THE OLD MAN COOKED RICE..

.. PEOPLE WOULD FLOCK TO HIS HOUSE.

COME IN, MY FRIENDS.

SOON THERE WERE SO MANY PEOPLE COMING EVERY DAY THAT HE BEGAN TO CHARGE A SMALL PRICE FOR THE RICE.

THE PEOPLE PAID WILLINGLY AND HE MADE A LOT OF MONEY.

THE CAT AND THE DOG TOO BECAME FAT WITH THE GOOD FOOD THEY ATE.

THIS IS THE SORT OF LIFE I LOVE. PLENTY TO EAT...

...AND NO WORK TO DO.

DAYS AND WEEKS PASSED. ONE MORNING HIS FIRST CUSTOMERS WERE SOME TRAVELLERS.

THEY BOUGHT A LOT OF RICE FROM HIM AND TOOK IT AWAY WITH THEM.

SOME TIME LATER AS THE OLD MAN WAS SERVING HIS OTHER CUSTOMERS —

ARE MY EYES DECEIVING ME? THE RICE SEEMS TO BE DIMINISHING.

WHEN HE HAD TAKEN OUT A FEW MORE LADLES —

THERE CAN BE NO DOUBT ABOUT IT NOW. THE QUANTITY HAS GREATLY DECREASED.

THE CONCH! WHERE IS THE CONCH?

OH, MY GOD! THE CONCH. IS GONE! IT MUST HAVE GONE WITH THE RICE I DOLED OUT TO THOSE TRAVELLERS.

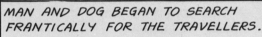

I'LL NEVER SEE THAT CONCH AGAIN.

HE HAS LOST THE CONCH!

OH, WHAT A SAD DAY!

WHEN THEY RETURNED HOME —

WHAT'S GOING ON? DON'T TELL ME SOMEONE RAN OFF WITHOUT PAYING.

YOU STUPID CREATURE! DO YOU THINK OUR MASTER WOULD RUN AFTER SOMEONE FOR A FEW COINS!

THE CONCH IS GONE! THE TRAVELLERS MUST HAVE GOT IT ALONG WITH THE RICE.

WHAT ARE YOU SAYING!

IF THE CONCH IS GONE, WE'LL HAVE TO STARVE!

THE VILLAGERS WONDERED WHY THE OLD MAN HAD STOPPED COOKING HIS DELECTABLE RICE. SOME OF THEM WHO WENT TO ENQUIRE CAME BACK WITH PUZZLED LOOKS ON THEIR FACES.

HE KEEPS MUMBLING ABOUT SOME CONCH.

WHAT DOES A CONCH HAVE TO DO WITH THE RICE?

HE'S GOING MAD, POOR FELLOW.

THE NEWS SPREAD THAT THE OLD MAN HAD TAKEN LEAVE OF HIS SENSES AND EVERYBODY BEGAN AVOIDING HIS HUT.

HE GOT ON FAIRLY WELL IN THE BEGINNING. HE HAD MONEY AND HE COULD BUY THE FOOD HE WANTED.

BUT IN COURSE OF TIME HIS MONEY BEGAN TO RUN OUT.

SEE HOW LITTLE WE'VE GOT TODAY.

WE'LL GET LESS TOMORROW. JUST WATCH.

IT'S NO USE GRUMBLING AND COMPLAINING.

IT'S TIME WE DID SOMETHING TO HELP OUR MASTER.

WHAT CAN WE DO?

I AM GOING TO SEARCH FOR THE CONCH. YOU MAY COME IF YOU WANT TO.

OH, THIS DOG!

HE ALWAYS WANTS TO DO SOMETHING. WHY CAN'T HE JUST WAIT AND SEE WHAT HAPPENS.

THE DOG TOOK THE CAT TO A RIVER.

WHY HAVE WE COME HERE?

I HAVE A FEELING THE TRAVELLERS CROSSED OVER TO THE OTHER SIDE. THAT'S WHY OUR MASTER AND I COULD NOT FIND THEM THAT DAY.

GET ON MY BACK. I'LL TAKE YOU ACROSS.

THE DOG SWAM WITH THE CAT TO THE OTHER SIDE.

NOW WE'LL SNIFF EVERY HUT IN THAT VILLAGE.

AS THE CAT AND THE DOG WENT ROUND—

I CAN GET A FAINT SMELL OF THE RICE THE CONCH USED TO PRODUCE.

IT SEEMS TO BE COMING FROM THAT WOODEN TRUNK.

YES, I CAN SMELL IT TOO! I THINK WE HAVE FOUND THE CONCH!

HOORAY!

WHAT ARE YOU WAITING FOR? GET IT OUT.

CAN'T YOU SEE THAT THE TRUNK IS LOCKED?

WE'LL HAVE TO BREAK INTO IT SOMEHOW. DO YOU THINK YOU COULD CATCH A RAT?

A RAT?

OF COURSE, I COULD! I AM OUT OF PRACTICE BUT... HUSH!

THERE'S ONE ...COMING OUT OF THAT HOLE!

EEEEE!

HAVE MERCY ON ME, FRIEND CAT. I HAVE A LARGE FAMILY TO LOOK AFTER.

PLEASE DON'T EAT ME.

WE WON'T HARM YOU IF YOU DO AS YOU ARE TOLD.

14

THERE'S A CONCH IN THAT TRUNK. WE WANT YOU TO TAKE IT OUT FOR US.

THAT SHOULD NOT BE DIFFICULT.

THEN GET TO WORK. WE WILL SET YOU FREE AS SOON AS YOU FINISH.

THE RAT BEGAN TO GNAW AT THE TRUNK.

AFTER SOME TIME —

LET GO OF MY TAIL. I CAN GO IN NOW.

SUDDENLY —

SOMEONE'S COMING.

WHAT'S THAT RAT DOING?

AH, HE'S PUSHING IT OUT.

WHAT'S GOING ON HERE?

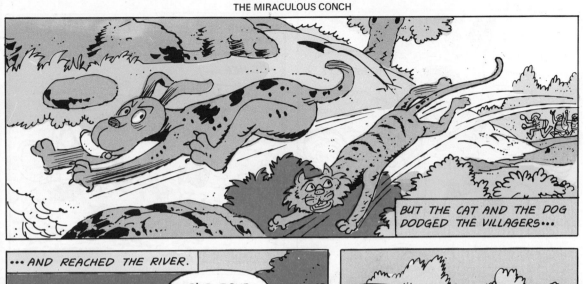

BUT THE CAT AND THE DOG DODGED THE VILLAGERS···

···AND REACHED THE RIVER.

WE'VE DONE IT! WE'VE GOT THE CONCH.

NOW GET ON MY BACK AND HOLD THE CONCH IN YOUR MOUTH.

AS THE DOG WAS SWIMMING TO THE OTHER SIDE WITH THE CAT—

HEY, LOOK AT THOSE TWO! DON'T THEY LOOK FUNNY?

HA HA HA!

17

HEARING THE CHILDREN LAUGH, THE CAT TOO FELT LIKE LAUGHING.

HEE HEE...

THE CONCH!

PLOP!!!

OH, YOU STUPID CAT!

THE DOG WENT AFTER THE CONCH, LEAVING THE CAT TO FEND FOR HERSELF.

HELP!

SHE DID NOT KNOW HOW TO SWIM. BUT SHE BEAT HER LEGS WILDLY IN ALL DIRECTIONS...

...AND SOMEHOW MANAGED TO REACH THE OTHER SIDE.

THIS IS WHAT HAPPENS WHEN YOU TRUST A DOG.

NOW I DARE NOT GO HOME. HE'LL BLAME ME FOR THE LOSS OF THE CONCH.

THE CAT CLIMBED A TREE AND HID HERSELF IN A HOLLOW.

I'LL STAY HERE FOR A FEW DAYS TILL HIS ANGER DIES DOWN.

MEANWHILE THE DOG HAD NOT BEEN ABLE TO RETRIEVE THE CONCH. HE SWAM ASHORE...

...AND RETURNED TO HIS MASTER.

WHEN THE OLD MAN SAW HIM —

WHERE DID YOU GO? AND WHERE IS THE CAT?

HAS SHE FOUND ANOTHER MASTER? OH, WELL! PERHAPS SHE HAS DONE THE RIGHT THING.

THE OLD MAN AND THE DOG SETTLED DOWN TO THEIR OLD LIFE.

SEVERAL DAYS PASSED. THEN ONE MORNING —

THERE'S NO FOOD AT ALL IN THE HOUSE TODAY.

I'LL GO DOWN TO THE RIVER AND SEE IF I CAN GET A FISH FROM ONE OF THE FISHER-MEN.

THE FISHERMEN HAD CAUGHT PLENTY OF FISH THAT DAY AND WHEN ONE OF THEM SAW THE DOG —

HERE, TAKE THIS TO YOUR MASTER.

WHAT A BIG FISH HE HAS GIVEN ME. THE MASTER WILL BE PLEASED.

THE OLD MAN WAS INDEED DELIGHTED.

I DON'T KNOW WHAT I WOULD HAVE DONE WITHOUT YOU!

NOW LET'S CLEAN AND COOK THIS MAGNIFICENT FISH.

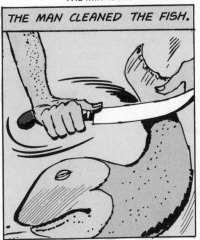

THE MAN CLEANED THE FISH.

WHEN HE CUT IT OPEN—

A CONCH!

I...I THINK IT'S THE SAME CONCH WHICH WE LOST.

WE HAVE GOT OUR CONCH BACK.

THE NEXT DAY—

IS MY NOSE DECEIVING ME OR...

IT ISN'T... I CAN SMELL IT TOO!

21

THE OLD MAN HAS BEGUN TO COOK THAT SPECIAL RICE AGAIN!

ONCE AGAIN PEOPLE BEGAN TO FLOCK TO THE OLD MAN'S HOUSE TO BUY RICE.

PLEASE NEVER STOP COOKING THIS DELIGHTFUL RICE AGAIN.

I WON'T.

MEAOW.

OH, IT'S YOU.

WELCOME HOME.

I FELT SO HOMESICK... I JUST HAD TO COME BACK.

DON'T TELL ME THAT! YOU MUST HAVE SMELT THE RICE.

THE CAT, THE DOG AND THEIR MASTER LIVED HAPPILY EVER AFTER.

A GAME OF CHESS

ONCE UPON A TIME THERE WAS A KING. HE WAS A DESPOT AND HE HAD A STRANGE METHOD OF ACQUIRING SLAVES.

ANYBODY WHO NEEDED HIS HELP HAD TO PLAY A GAME OF CHESS WITH HIM.

I AM NOT VERY GOOD AT THIS GAME, YOUR MAJESTY.

THAT DOESN'T MATTER.

IT'S NOT YOUR SKILL, BUT THIS CAT'S THAT WILL DECIDE THE OUTCOME OF THE GAME.

CAT?

IF SHE MOVES AND DROPS EVEN ONE OF THE SEVEN LAMPS BEING PLACED ON HER TAIL, I SHALL GRANT WHATEVER YOU REQUEST.

BUT IF SHE SHOULD SIT WITHOUT MOVING TILL THE END OF THE GAME, YOU SHALL BECOME MY SLAVE.

SHALL WE START?

UNFORTUNATELY FOR ANYONE WHO PLAYED AGAINST THE KING, THE CAT WAS WELL TRAINED. SO THE KING NEVER LOST.

YOU ARE NOW MY SLAVE...

ULP!

ONE DAY A MERCHANT FROM A DISTANT CITY CAME TO THE PALACE.

I HAVE COME TO ASK PERMISSION TO TRADE IN THIS CITY.

CAN YOU PLAY CHESS?

OH, YES! I AM VERY GOOD AT IT, IN FACT. BUT WHY DO YOU ASK?

WHEN THE MINISTER EXPLAINED WHY —

WHAT A STRANGE RULE! YOU HAVE TO PLAY CHESS WITH THE KING BEFORE YOU CAN ASK A FAVOUR OF HIM.

WELL...?

TAKE ME TO THE KING.

I HAVE COME A LONG DISTANCE AND I CANNOT GO BACK EMPTY-HANDED.

SOME TIME LATER, THE MERCHANT SAT DOWN TO PLAY WITH THE KING.

HE DID EVERYTHING POSSIBLE TO PROLONG THE GAME.

IT WENT ON AND ON.

BUT FINALLY, TO HIS HORROR —

I HAVE WON. THE GAME IS OVER AND THE CAT HAS NOT MOVED!

I AM DONE FOR.

I'LL HAVE TO SEND A MESSAGE TO MY WIFE EXPLAINING MY PLIGHT.

THE MERCHANT'S WIFE WAS A BRAVE AND CLEVER WOMAN. WHEN SHE GOT THE NEWS OF HER HUSBAND'S MISFORTUNE—

I MUST SECURE HIS FREEDOM SOMEHOW...

...AND TEACH THAT WICKED KING A LESSON. HOW DARE HE LET A CAT DECIDE MY HUSBAND'S FATE!

CAT! THAT GIVES ME AN IDEA.

DRESSING HERSELF UP AS A MAN, THE WOMAN WENT TO THE PALACE WITH ONE OF HER SERVANTS.

NOW DO EXACTLY AS I'VE TOLD YOU.

YES, MADAM.

I HAVE COME TO ASK A FAVOUR OF THE KING.

YOU MAY ASK HIM FOR ANYTHING.

26

27

THE GAME BEGAN. THE KING PLAYED CONFIDENTLY.

THIS MAN TOO WILL SOON BE MY SLAVE.

AFTER SOME TIME, THE SERVANT WHO WAS STANDING OUTSIDE···

...RELEASED A MOUSE INTO THE PLAYING ROOM.

ON SEEING THE MOUSE, THE CAT STIFFENED AND PRICKED UP HER EARS.

!

BUT THE KING GLARED FIERCELY AT HER AND SHE MADE HERSELF IMMOBILE AGAIN.

A LITTLE LATER, THE SERVANT LET OUT ANOTHER MOUSE.

AGAIN THE CAT MOVED RESTLESSLY...

...AND ALMOST DROPPED A LAMP.

I'D BETTER END THE GAME FAST. SOMETHING IS WRONG WITH THAT CAT TODAY.

THE KING IS DESPERATE. NOW I MUST BE ALERT. THANK GOD MY HUSBAND TAUGHT ME ALL THE TRICKY MOVES!

AS THE KING TRIED FRANTICALLY TO FINISH THE GAME...

...THE SERVANT LET OUT A THIRD MOUSE.

THIS TIME THE CAT COULD NOT RESTRAIN HERSELF. SHE JUMPED FORWARD, UPSETTING ALL THE LAMPS.

I HAVE WON. THE CAT HAS MOVED AND THE GAME HAS NOT ENDED.

WHAT DO YOU WANT FROM ME?

I WANT YOU TO RELEASE ALL THE MEN YOU HAVE ENSLAVED.

THE KING HAD TO GRANT HER REQUEST AND THE WOMAN WAS SOON REUNITED WITH HER HUSBAND.

Available on the iPad!

A chemical engineer by profession, Anant Pai gave up his job to follow his dream, a dream that led to the birth of Amar Chitra Katha and Tinkle.

Anant Pai - Master Storyteller traces the story of the man who left behind a legacy of learning and laughter for children. ACK Media's new iPad app brings alive a new reading experience using panel-by-panel view technology, created in-house.

THE GOLDEN SAND

FOLK TALES FROM NEPAL

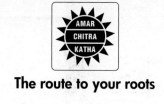

The route to your roots

THE GOLDEN SAND

When Sakhwal accidentally gets some sand, intended for the king, he has no idea that it will turn to gold and change his life.

Dravyashah uses his wits to win the kingdom of Liglig in the Himalayas. He is horrified when his brother demands the kingdom from him. When Dravyashah refuses to give up his kingdom, it looks like war will break out between the two brothers and their kingdoms.

The stories in this collection come from the mountain country of Nepal. Though Nepal is very close to India and shares so much of its culture, these stories have a flavour all their own.

Script
Dr. Kashiraj Upadhyaya

Illustrations
Dilip Kadam

Editor
Anant Pai

THE GOLDEN SAND

WHEN SAKHWAL, A SAND-MERCHANT OF KATHMANDU, STEPPED OUT OF HIS HOUSE ONE MORNING, HE SAW TWO LABOURERS COME BY.

I'LL TAKE THAT SAND. I'LL PAY YOU WELL FOR IT.

IT'S FOR... FOR...

WE'LL GIVE IT TO YOU, SIR.

BUT WHAT ABOUT...

SSSH! WE CAN ALWAYS GO BACK AND GET SOME MORE FOR THE KING.

THE MEN WENT INTO SAKHWAL'S WAREHOUSE AND EMPTIED THEIR BASKETS.

THANK YOU. HERE'S THE MONEY FOR THE SAND.

THEN THEY WENT BACK TO LAKHU, THE PILGRIM CENTRE SITUATED AT THE CONFLUENCE OF THE RIVERS BHATIKHU AND VISHNUMATI, REFILLED THEIR BASKETS...

...AND CARRIED THEM...

...TO THE PALACE OF THE KING OF BHADGAO*.

WE HAVE BROUGHT THE SAND, MAHARAJ.

GOOD! PUT IT DOWN IN THERE.

* A NEIGHBOURING STATE

A FEW HOURS LATER—

NO!

IT IS STILL SAND! MERE SAND!

THE KING EXAMINED THE CONTENTS OF ALL THE BASKETS.

HUMPH! NOTHING BUT SAND.

HE SENT FOR THE COURT ASTROLOGER.

YOU CLAIMED THAT THE SAND OF LAKHU COLLECTED AT A CERTAIN AUSPICIOUS MOMENT WOULD TURN INTO GOLD AFTER TWELVE HOURS.

IS THIS YOUR GOLD?

WHAT COULD HAVE GONE WRONG? I WAS SO SURE...

MEANWHILE, AT SAKHWAL'S WAREHOUSE—

WHY IS THE SAND SHINING SO?

WH... WHAT'S THIS? OH! OH! WONDER OF WONDERS!

IT'S GOLD DUST!

I'D BETTER PUT IT AWAY IN A BIN.

BUT THAT NIGHT SAKHWAL WAS RACKED BY DOUBTS.

IT'S TRUE I FOUND IT IN MY WAREHOUSE... BUT DOES THAT MAKE IT MINE? SHOULD I KEEP IT OR SHOULD I... OH, WELL, I'LL SLEEP OVER IT AND THEN DECIDE.

THE NEXT MORNING HE SET OUT OF HIS HOUSE.

HE WAS WALKING THROUGH THE MARKET-PLACE, STILL STRUGGLING WITH HIS PROBLEM...

...WHEN A VOICE BEHIND HIM BROKE INTO HIS THOUGHTS.

MERCY! MERCY, SAHUJI.

SAKHWAL SLOWLY TURNED ROUND.

PLEASE DON'T TAKE AWAY MY LAND AND MY CATTLE, SAHUJI. I'LL BE RUINED!

GRANT ME SOME MORE TIME! PLEASE! I PROMISE I'LL PAY EVERY SINGLE COIN!

SO HAD YOU PROMISED— LAST MONTH, AND THE MONTH BEFORE!

NO, I CAN'T WAIT ANY MORE! PAY NOW OR ELSE I'LL...

SAKHWAL IMAGINED HIMSELF IN THE OLD MAN'S PLIGHT.

AND HE KNEW WHAT HE MUST DO.

HERE! TAKE THIS AND GIVE HIM BACK HIS BOND.

YOU...!

YOU... LOW-BORN...

I MAY BE LOW-BORN, I MAY BE IMPURE...

...BUT MY GOLD IS NEITHER. SO TAKE IT!

6

THE MONEY-LENDER ACCEPTED THE GOLD AND RETURNED THE BOND TO THE POOR CREDITOR.

MAY GOD BLESS... HE'S GONE!

BAPUJI...

BUT SAKHWAL WAS ALREADY OUT OF EARSHOT.

THE SCENE HE HAD JUST WITNESSED SET HIM THINKING.

THERE MUST BE HUNDREDS LIKE HIM...

...WHO ARE CAUGHT IN THE CLUTCHES OF MERCILESS MONEY-LENDERS... HM-M-M...

HE WENT STRAIGHT TO THE COURT OF KING JAYADEVA MALLA.

SALUTATIONS, MAHARAJ!

I HAVE SOMETHING TO TELL YOU, MAHARAJ.

YES? GO AHEAD.

WELL... ER... I... I BOUGHT SOME SAND YESTERDAY. AND NEARLY TWELVE HOURS LATER...

WHEN HE FINISHED HIS TALE...

MAHARAJ, I WANT TO USE THE GOLD TO FREE ALL THOSE WHO ARE UNFORTUNATE ENOUGH TO BE IN THE CLUTCHES OF MONEY-LENDERS.

DO I HAVE YOUR PERMISSION, MAHARAJ? AND YOUR BLESSINGS?

BLESSINGS? PERMISSION?

MY GOOD MAN, MEN RICHER AND MIGHTIER THAN YOU WOULD HAVE KEPT THE GOLD FOR THEMSELVES...

...AND YOU ARE READY TO PART WITH IT SO THAT OTHERS MAY BE FREE OF DEBT!

PERMIT ME TO SALUTE YOU, NOBLE SAKHWAL!

THEN THE KING TURNED TO HIS COURTIERS.

A MAN LIKE SAKHWAL IS RARE. HIS NAME SHOULD DESCRIBE HIS NATURE.

FROM TODAY, HE SHALL BE KNOWN AS SHANKHDHAR — AFTER LORD VISHNU, THE DIVINE PROTECTOR.

SHANKHDHAR KO JAI*!

SHANKHDHAR KO JAI!

* NEPALI EQUIVALENT OF 'KI JAI'

AND TO MARK THIS GREAT OCCASION, THE CALENDAR WE FOLLOW HENCEFORTH SHALL BE THE SHANKHDHAR SAMVAT, OF WHICH THIS GREAT DAY SHALL BE THE FIRST.

MAHARAJ JAYADEVA KO JAI!

LONG LIVE SHANKHDHAR!

WHEN SHANKHDHAR'S OFFER WAS PROCLAIMED, PEOPLE FROM FAR AND NEAR APPROACHED HIM. AND HE HELPED ONE AND ALL.

SOON—

NOBODY CAME TODAY! THERE IS NOT A SINGLE DEBT-RIDDEN SOUL IN THE LAND! AHA!

ONE DAY THE KING SENT FOR SAKHWAL.

WILL YOU COME WITH ME TO THE TEMPLE OF PASHUPATINATH*?

GLADLY, MAHARAJ.

* SHIVA

WHEN THEY ARRIVED AT THE ENTRANCE—

COME IN, SHANKHDHAR.

B...BUT... MAHARAJ...

...HOW CAN I, ENTER THE SACRED TEMPLE?

PLEASE GO IN, MAHARAJ. I'LL BOW TO THE LORD FROM OUT HERE.

SHANKHDHAR!

12

THE MOTHER

THE PEOPLE OF LIGLIG* WILL SOON BE HOLDING THEIR ANNUAL RACE TO CHOOSE THEIR NEW KING FOR THE YEAR.

AND WHAT A RACE! RUNNING UPHILL AND DOWNHILL!

DRAVYASHAH, THE YOUNGER BROTHER OF NARHARISHAH, KING OF LAMJUNG@ WAS AN ADVENTUROUS, FEARLESS AND AMBITIOUS YOUNG MAN.

WHAT MAKES THEM THINK THAT A PERSON WHO CAN RUN FAST WILL MAKE A GOOD KING?

WHAT LIGLIG NEEDS IS A KING WHO IS WISE AND VALIANT.

IN THAT CASE YOU WOULD BE THE IDEAL RULER.

BUT I AM NO GOOD AT RUNNING.

WHO SAYS YOU HAVE TO BE? I HAVE A PLAN. LISTEN...

*A STATE IN NEPAL   @ A STATE BORDERING LIGLIG

13

THE THREE FRIENDS RODE TO LIGLIG ON DUSSEHRA DAY, THE DAY OF THE GREAT RACE.

THE RACE BEGAN AT THE FOOT OF THE HILL.

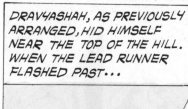

DRAVYASHAH, AS PREVIOUSLY ARRANGED, HID HIMSELF NEAR THE TOP OF THE HILL. WHEN THE LEAD RUNNER FLASHED PAST...

...HE JOINED IN...

...OVERTOOK THE RUNNER...

...REACHED THE TEMPLE ATOP THE HILL...

...RECEIVED THE GARLAND FROM THE UNSUSPECTING PRIEST...

...AND RAN DOWNHILL...

...TO THE WAITING CROWD.

CONGRATULATIONS, YOUNG MAN! WHAT'S YOUR NAME?

DRAVYASHAH, SIR.

YOU SHALL BE OUR KING FOR THIS YEAR. RAJA DRAVYASHAH KO JAI!

RAJA DRAVYASHAH KO JAI!

DRAVYASHAH WAS TAKEN IN PROCESSION...

...TO THE PALACE...

...AND INSTALLED ON THE THRONE.

WHAT IS YOUR FIRST COMMAND, MAHARAJ?

WELL...

...FROM NOW ON, THE CUSTOM OF SELECTING A KING EVERY YEAR SHALL BE STOPPED FORTHWITH.

UNDER ONE PERMANENT KING, LIGLIG WILL PROSPER AND FLOURISH.

17

DRAVYASHAH THEN MADE A VISIT TO LAMJUNG TO MEET HIS MOTHER, BASANTVATI.

SALUTATIONS, MOTHER! WITH YOUR BLESSINGS YOUR YOUNGER SON TOO HAS BECOME A KING TODAY.

MAY GOD BLESS YOU, MY SON.

THEN HE WENT TO NARHARISHAH WHO HAD ALREADY HEARD THE NEWS.

WELL DONE, DRAVYA! YOU HAVE BROUGHT GLORY TO LAMJUNG— AND TO ME!

I, THE LORD OF LAMJUNG, WILL BE THE LORD OF LIGLIG TOO! MY TREASURY WILL NOW OVERFLOW, MY...

PARDON ME FOR INTERRUPTING YOU, BROTHER.

AS MY ELDER BROTHER, YOU ARE NO DOUBT THE MASTER OF THE KINGDOM WE INHERITED FROM OUR FATHER.

BUT THE KINGDOM I HAVE WON SHALL BE MINE AND MINE ALONE.

AND DRAVYASHAH WALKED OUT.

YOU ARE DRUNK WITH SUCCESS!

GO HOME AND THINK IT OVER!

DRAVYASHAH RETURNED TO HIS CAPITAL...

...RAISED AN ARMY...

...AND EXTENDED HIS TERRITORY.

THEN ONE DAY HE RECEIVED A MESSAGE FROM HIS ELDER BROTHER.

KING NARHARISHAH SENDS HIS CONGRATULATIONS ON YOUR VICTORY, SIR.

AND HE WANTS TO REMIND YOU ABOUT THE TRIBUTE DUE TO HIM.

WHAT TRIBUTE?

PLEASE TELL MY BROTHER THAT WHILE I THANK HIM FOR HIS CONGRATULA- TIONS...

...THERE IS NO QUESTION OF MY PAYING ANY TRIBUTE.

I HAD MADE IT CLEAR TO HIM LONG AGO.

* AROUND JANUARY-FEBRUARY

WHEN THE MONTH OF MAGHA CAME ROUND, KING NARHARISHAH SET OUT WITH THE QUEEN MOTHER AND HIS FAMILY FOR THE ANNUAL DIP IN THE RIVER CHEPE.

SO DID KING DRAVYASHAH.

THEY SOON ARRIVED AT THE BANKS OF THE RIVER.

DRAVYASHAH WAS ABOUT TO CROSS IT, WHEN—

MY LORD! DON'T GO ALONE. TAKE SOME SOLDIERS WITH YOU.

SOLDIERS? WHY?

WELL... ER... JUST IN CASE...

DON'T BE RIDICULOUS. I AM GOING TO ASK THEIR BLESSINGS.

DRAVYASHAH CROSSED THE RIVER...

...AND WALKED TOWARDS BASANTVATI.

MAY YOU LIVE LONG, SON. MAY YOU ACHIEVE GREATER GLORIES!

THEN AS HE TURNED TO NARHARISHAH, THE ELDER BROTHER BACKED AWAY.

WHY, BROTHER?

I SEEK YOUR BLESSINGS, BROTHER!

NARHARISHAH ANSWERED HIM WITH A HOSTILE STARE.

24

DRAVYASHAH FELL AT HIS MOTHER'S FEET...

...AND WALKED TO THE OTHER SIDE OF THE RIVER.

IF YOU WANT TO EXTEND YOUR KINGDOM, DO SO TOWARDS THE EAST. DON'T EVER CROSS CHEPE AND COME TOWARDS MY RIGHT.

MAY GOD BE WITH YOU, MY SON!

THEN SHE CALLED OUT TO NARHARISHAH.

AND YOU, SON, ARE FREE TO EXTEND YOUR KINGDOM TOWARDS THE WEST. BUT...

...NEVER, EVER DREAM OF CROSSING THE RIVER TO EXTEND YOUR KINGDOM TOWARDS THE EAST."

MY SONS ARE BRAVE! THEY CAN CONQUER THE WORLD. BUT REMEMBER...

...CHEPE IS YOUR MOTHER. CROSSING HER WOULD MEAN TRAMPLING ON YOUR MOTHER'S BOSOM. NEVER DO THAT.

THE TWO BROTHERS RETURNED TO THEIR STATES, AND THE BATTLE WAS AVERTED.

MANY DECADES LATER, PRITHVINARAYAN SHAH, A DESCENDANT OF DRAVYASHAH, UNITED THE TWO STATES, AND THE NEW COUNTRY CAME TO BE KNOWN AS NEPAL.

THE KINGDOM OF NEPAL

Script : Swarn Khandpur
Illustrations : S. K. Parab

THE HIMALAYAN KINGDOM OF NEPAL HAS SOME OF THE HIGHEST MOUNTAINS IN THE WORLD. THE MIGHTIEST AMONG THEM IS MOUNT EVEREST WHICH THE NEPALESE VENERATE AS THE 'TALLEST GODDESS' IN THE WORLD.

IN THE TEMPERATE FORESTS OF THESE MOUNTAINS, THE RHODODENDRON SHRUBS GROW AS TALL AS TREES—SOMETIMES 15 METRES HIGH ! NO WONDER THE RHODODENDRON IS THE NATIONAL FLOWER OF NEPAL. ALONG THE SOUTHERN BORDER OF NEPAL LIE THE DENSE SWAMPY JUNGLES OF THE TERAI. THIS REGION IS RICH IN WILD LIFE.

UNTIL THE 18TH CENTURY, NEPAL WAS MADE UP OF A NUMBER OF SMALL PRINCIPALITIES. IT WAS UNITED UNDER ONE RULE BY PRITHVI NARAYAN SHAH WITH HIS GURKHA SOLDIERS.
THE GURKHAS DERIVE THEIR NAME FROM THE TOWN OF GORKHA IN NEPAL. BRAVE AND LOYAL, THEY ARE RESPECTED THE WORLD OVER FOR THEIR VALOUR.
A GURKHA ALWAYS CARRIES THE 'KUKRI' THE TRADITIONAL NEPALESE KNIFE.

THE HARDY SHERPAS, LIKE THE GURKHAS, ARE WORLD FAMOUS AS GUIDES TO MOUNTAINEERING ENTHUSIASTS.
TENZING NORGAY WHO SCALED MOUNT EVEREST WITH EDMUND HILLARY FOR THE FIRST TIME ON MAY 29, 1953 WAS A SHERPA.

28

KATHMANDU IS THE CAPITAL OF NEPAL. HERE STANDS THE FAMOUS TEMPLE OF PASHUPATINATH DEDICATED TO SHIVA. ON MAHASHIVARATRI DAY, A LARGE NUMBER OF PILGRIMS VISIT THE SHRINE.

THE PAGODA STYLE OF ARCHITECTURE ORIGINATED IN NEPAL FROM THERE, IT SPREAD TO SOUTH EAST ASIA.

ANOTHER VERY SACRED PLACE FOR THE HINDUS IS NARAYANTHAN. HERE IN THE MIDDLE OF A POND LORD VISHNU RECLINES ON A MANY-HEADED SERPENT. NEPAL IS THE ONLY HINDU KINGDOM IN THE WORLD. THE KINGS ARE REGARDED AS INCARNATIONS OF LORD VISHNU.

THIS BUDDHIST SHRINE OF SWAYAMBHUNATH IS BELIEVED TO BE MORE THAN 2,000 YEARS OLD. GAUTAMA THE BUDDHA WAS BORN IN

THE SOUTHERN PART OF NEPAL, CLOSE TO THE INDIAN BORDER.

BUDDHISM, THEREFORE, IS AN IMPORTANT RELIGION OF NEPAL. IN THIS TERRACOTTA TEMPLE OF MAHABUDDHA AT PATAN, EVERY BRICK BEARS THE IMAGE OF THE ENLIGHTENED ONE. PATAN, WHICH WAS KNOWN AS LALITPUR IN THE PAST, HAS LONG BEEN FAMOUS FOR ITS CARVINGS IN STONE AND METAL.

30

THE CLEVER DANCER

A BATTLE OF WITS

THE CLEVER DANCER

Though very young, Muladeva is regarded as one of the wisest men in Ujjaini.

One day, he sets off for Patliputra, with his friend Shashi, eager to debate with the scholars there. On the outskirts of the city, they meet a girl picking mangoes. She and Muladeva start arguing but the girl outwits him with ease and then, disappears.

Enchanted by her quick replies and her intelligence Muladeva decides that he will not rest until he has found her, outsmarted her, and married her.

In this story from the Kathasaritsagar, Muladeva's quest results in an elaborate and prolonged battle of wits.

Script
Jagjit Uppal

Illustrations
Madhu Powle

Editor
Anant Pai

THE CLEVER DANCER

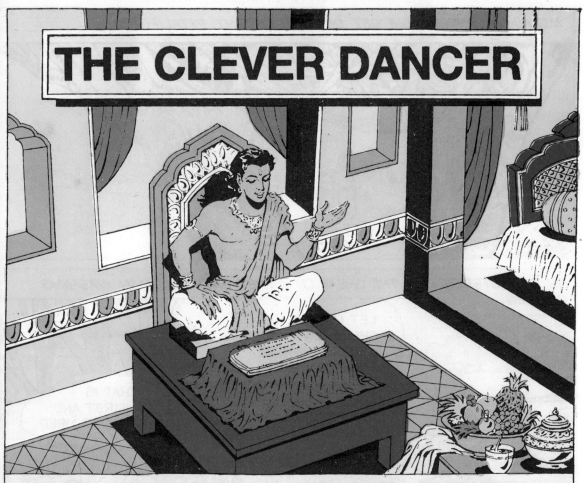

MULADEVA WAS A YOUNG BRAHMIN OF UJJAINI. HE WAS A MAN OF GREAT KNOWLEDGE AND INGENUITY. HE DEFEATED PUNDITS AND SCHOLARS IN DEBATES UPON THE SCRIPTURES, AND WAS CONSIDERED AN AUTHORITY ON THE VEDAS.

MULADEVA HAD A CLOSE FRIEND CALLED SHASHI. ONE DAY SHASHI CAME TO MULADEVA WITH A SUGGESTION.

YOU ARE A MASTER IN THE ART OF ORATORY AND YOUR FAME HAS TRAVELLED FAR AND WIDE. WHY NOT GO TO PATALIPUTRA AND EARN GREATER GLORY?

A FINE SUGGESTION, FRIEND. AND I CAN TEST MY METTLE IN THAT HOME OF POLISHED WIT AND REFINEMENT.

MULADEVA AND SHASHI SET OUT FOR DISTANT PATALIPUTRA.

ON THE OUTSKIRTS OF THE GREAT CITY, THEY SAW A WOMAN WASHING CLOTHES.

LET US ASK HER IF SHE KNOWS OF SOME PLACE WHERE WE CAN STAY.

THAT IS OUR FIRST AND FOREMOST NEED.

THEY APPROACHED THE WOMAN.

GOOD LADY, WHERE DO TRAVELLERS FIND LODGING?

I KNOW THAT DUCKS NEST ON THE RIVER BANKS, FISH IN THE WATER, BEES IN LOTUSES; BUT I HAVEN'T THE FAINTEST IDEA WHERE TRAVELLERS STAY!

MULADEVA AND SHASHI WERE DUMBFOUNDED.

WHAT DO WE DO NOW?

JUST WALK INTO THE CITY, FRIEND.

THEY HAD HARDLY GONE A FEW YARDS, WHEN THEY FOUND A BOY CRYING AT THE DOOR OF A HOUSE, WITH A PLATE OF WARM RICE-PUDDING IN FRONT OF HIM.

ONLY A FOOLISH CHILD WEEPS WHEN SUCH DELICIOUS HOT FOOD IS BEFORE HIM.

I AGREE.

THE LITTLE BOY BURST OUT LAUGHING.

ONLY FOOLS WILL NOT UNDERSTAND WHY I CRY. I HAVE TO WAIT FOR THE PUDDING TO COOL BEFORE I CAN EAT IT; BY CRYING, MY THROAT IS CLEARED AND MY LUNGS GET EXERCISE. BUT COUNTRY BUMPKINS LIKE YOU CANNOT UNDERSTAND ALL THIS!

THE FRIENDS WERE SHOCKED AT HIS LANGUAGE.

SUCH WORDS FROM THE MOUTH OF A LITTLE BOY!

WHAT A PRECOCIOUS CHILD!

AS THEY WERE CROSSING A FOREST

GIVE US SOME MANGOES, FAIR ONE.

HOT OR COLD ?

THE FRIENDS EXCHANGED GLANCES.

ANSWER THAT, MULADEVA.

MULADEVA WAS READY WITH HIS REPLY.

SOME WARM ONES FIRST.

SHE THREW DOWN SOME MANGOES.

MULADEVA AND SHASHI PICKED UP THE FRUIT, AND BLEW THE DUST OFF THEM.

AFTER THEY HAD EATEN THOSE MANGOES

WERE THEY TOO WARM? I NOTICED YOU BLEW ON THEM. THEY ARE QUITE COOL — YOU CAN SAVE YOUR BREATH.

BY NOW MULADEVA, THE GREAT WIT, WAS FEELING HUMBLED, EVEN ASHAMED.

SHE IS THE WITTIEST CREATURE I'VE MET. I'LL GET THIS CLEVER GIRL FOR A WIFE AND TEACH HER A LESSON OR TWO.

SHASHI, WE MUST FIND OUT WHERE SHE LIVES.

THAT EVENING—

MULADEVA, SHE IS THE DAUGHTER OF A RICH BRAHMIN NAMED YAJNASWAMI.

WE MUST ACT PROMPTLY.

THE FOLLOWING DAY, MULADEVA AND SHASHI DISGUISED THEMSELVES AS HUMBLE BRAHMINS AND STARTED OFF FOR YAJNASWAMI'S HOUSE.

NO ONE WILL RECOGNIZE US!

THEY SAT OPPOSITE HER HOUSE AND BEGAN TO RECITE VERSES FROM THE VEDAS.

AFTER A WHILE, HER FATHER CAME OUT OF THE HOUSE.

THEY APPEAR TO BE LEARNED BRAHMINS.

HE APPROACHED THEM.

GOOD SIR, WHERE DO YOU COME FROM?

FROM THE CITY OF MAYAPURI. WE HAVE COME HERE TO STUDY THE SCRIPTURES AND ANCIENT LORE.

THE RICH AND NOBLE YAJNASWAMI TOOK AN INSTANT LIKING TO MULADEVA.

PLEASE BE MY GUESTS FOR THE NEXT FOUR MONTHS. YOU HAVE TRAVELLED A LONG WAY.

BETTER THAN WE EXPECTED!

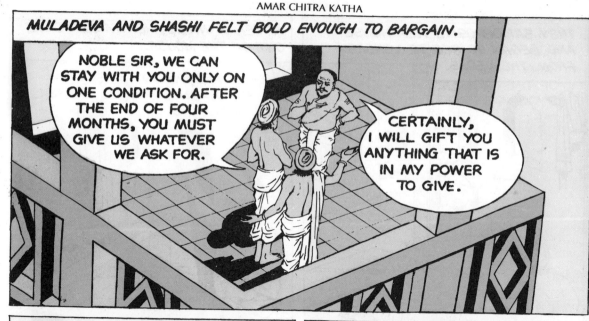

MULADEVA AND SHASHI FELT BOLD ENOUGH TO BARGAIN.

NOBLE SIR, WE CAN STAY WITH YOU ONLY ON ONE CONDITION. AFTER THE END OF FOUR MONTHS, YOU MUST GIVE US WHATEVER WE ASK FOR.

CERTAINLY, I WILL GIFT YOU ANYTHING THAT IS IN MY POWER TO GIVE.

MULADEVA AND SHASHI LIVED IN YAJNASWAMI'S HOUSE. THEY ENCOUNTERED YAJNASWAMI'S DAUGHTER A NUMBER OF TIMES BUT SHE DID NOT RECOGNISE THEM IN THEIR DISGUISE.

AS INNOCENT AS A FLOWER! BUT I CAN'T FORGET THAT SHE HAD THE BETTER OF ME!

AT THE END OF FOUR MONTHS

WE THANK YOU FOR YOUR KIND HOSPITALITY.

IT WAS A PLEASURE TO HAVE SUCH STIMULATING COMPANY.

9

YAJNASWAMI'S DAUGHTER AND MULADEVA WERE MARRIED.

ALONE IN THE BRIDAL CHAMBER

DO YOU RECOGNISE ME? THOSE WARM AND COOL MANGOES...

SHE BROKE INTO A SMILE.

COUNTRY BUMPKINS ARE TOO SLOW FOR CITY WITS.

I, THE COUNTRY BUMPKIN, AM ABOUT TO DESERT YOU AND GO FAR AWAY. AND YOU, THE CITY WIT, WILL STAY HERE AND FRET!

MULADEVA'S WIFE SHOWED NO SIGN OF ALARM OR FEAR BUT INSTEAD, THREW HER HUSBAND A CHALLENGE.

YOU WILL COME BACK TO ME AS FATHER OF MY SON!

DEAR EXPERT AT REPARTEE AND RIDDLE, LET US SEE HOW YOU DO THAT.

AFTER THESE EXCHANGES, THE TIRED PAIR WENT TO SLEEP.

IN THE DEAD OF NIGHT, MULADEVA GOT UP.

I SHALL SLIP THIS RING ON TO HER FINGER BEFORE I LEAVE HER.

MULADEVA MET SHASHI OUTSIDE THE HOUSE AS PLANNED AND TOGETHER THEY LEFT FOR UJJAINI.

THE NEXT DAY

SO, MY GOOD HUSBAND WAS NOT JOKING. HE DID LEAVE.

SEEING THE RING ON HER FINGER

HIS NAME IS EN-GRAVED ON THIS RING THE RENOWNED MULA DEVA OF UJJAINI! I WILL GO THERE AND PROVE THAT I WAS NOT JOKING EITHER!

SHE WENT TO HER FATHER.

FATHER, MY HUSBAND HAS DESERTED ME. WISH TO LEAVE ON A PILGRIMAGE.

MY CHILD, I UNDER STAND.

SHE TOOK PERMISSION FROM HER FATHER AND SET OUT FOR UJJAINI, EQUIPPED WITH MONEY AND ATTENDANTS.

ON THE WAY SHE BOUGHT HERSELF A FINE COSTUME AND....

...DRESSED AS A DANCER, SHE APPROACHED UJJAINI WITH MUCH FANFARE.

A CHARMING WOMAN.

A PRINCESS!

SHE CAMPED OUTSIDE THE CITY AND HER SERVANTS WENT ABOUT PROCLAIMING HER AS THE LOVELIEST WOMAN IN THE WORLD.

WHO IS YOUR MISTRESS?

SHE IS THE LADY SUMANGALA FROM THE CITY OF KAMARUPA.

A DISTINGUISHED DANCER OF UJJAINI, NAMED DEVADATTA, APPROACHED SUMANGALA.

I HAVE HEARD GRAND REPORTS OF YOU AS A DANCER. I AM A DANCER TOO.

I TOO HAVE HEARD THAT UJJAINI IS A PLACE OF GREAT CULTURE AND HAVE COME TO SEE FOR MYSELF.

PLEASE BE MY GUEST.

SUMANGALA ACCEPTED THE OFFER. DEVADATTA. GAVE SUMANGALA HER OWN MANSION TO LIVE IN.

NEWS ABOUT SUMANGALA'S CHARM AND BEAUTY REACHED SHASHI'S EARS

A LOVELY DANCER FROM KAMARUPA! I SHOULD LIKE TO MEET HER.

SHASHI SENT A MESSENGER TO SUMANGALA.

MY MASTER SENDS HIS GREETINGS TO YOU AND THESE PRESENTS TOO.

TELL YOUR MASTER THAT I DO NOT SET MUCH STORE BY PRESENTS. AS FOR HIS GREETINGS, I WISH HE HAD COME WITH THEM IN PERSON.

THE MESSENGER RETURNED TO SHASHI.

I SHALL SEE HER THIS EVENING.

THAT NIGHT, SHASHI LEFT FOR HER PALACE, DRESSED IN FINE CLOTHES.

WHEN HE CAME TO THE FIRST ENTRANCE OF THE PALACE, THE DOORKEEPER STOPPED HIM.

SIR, YOU MAY HAVE HAD A BATH AT HOME, BUT TO ENTER, YOU MUST BATHE HERE ONCE AGAIN. ELSE YOU MAY NOT GO IN.

THE SURPRISED SHASHI AGREED AND WAS LED TO A TASTEFULLY DECORATED BATH.

FEMALE SERVANTS WAITED UPON HIM AND BY THE TIME HE FINISHED BATHING, THE FIRST WATCH OF THE NIGHT HAD PASSED.

SHASHI THEN ENTERED THE SECOND PORTAL OF THE PALACE.

YOU HAVE HAD A BATH, BUT UNLESS YOU ARE DRESSED IN STYLE YOU MAY NOT GO IN.

SHASHI TURNED BACK AND WAS SOON ADORNED IN BEAUTIFUL GARMENTS BY SUMANGALA'S FEMALE SERVANTS. BY THIS TIME THE SECOND WATCH OF THE NIGHT HAD COME TO AN END.

AT THE THIRD PORTAL HE WAS ASKED TO PARTAKE OF A DAINTY MEAL.
THIS FURTHER DELAYED SHASHI, AND THE THIRD WATCH OF THE NIGHT
HAD ALSO PASSED.

WHEN SHASHI ENTERED THE FOURTH AND FINAL DOOR THAT LED TO
SUMANGALA'S PRIVATE APARTMENT, THE DOORKEEPER STOPPED HIM
RUDELY.

A FINE GENTLEMAN
YOU ARE TO VISIT A LADY
AT THIS UNEARTHLY HOUR!
GO AWAY, GOOD SIR, OR
YOU'LL DRAG MISFORTUNE
UPON YOUR HEAD!

CRESTFALLEN, SHASHI
RETURNED HOME.

THE LADY
SUMANGALA SEEMS
TO BE GIFTED
WITH SHREWD
INTELLIGENCE.

THE NEXT DAY SHASHI WENT TO MULADEVA AND RELATED THE INCIDENT.

OUTDONE BY A MERE DANCER! FRIEND, I SWEAR TO GET THE BETTER OF THIS WOMAN.

THAT NIGHT MULADEVA WENT TO SUMANGALA'S PALACE, CARRYING A NUMBER OF PRECIOUS GIFTS.

WHEN HE WAS STOPPED AT THE FIRST DOOR, HE BRIBED THE DOORKEEPER WITH A VALUABLE PIECE OF JEWELLERY.

A CASKET OF GOLD STUDDED WITH PEARLS, ALL FOR YOU.

HE WAS SOON PERMITTED TO PASS THE DOOR.

IN THE SAME WAY HE GAINED ADMITTANCE THROUGH THE OTHER DOORS.

AT SUMANGALA'S DOOR HE GAVE THE DOORKEEPER A NECKLACE MADE OF BRILLIANT DIAMONDS.

GIVE YOUR MISTRESS THIS AND SAY THAT MULADEVA WAITS UPON HER.

MULADEVA WAS SOON IN THE PRESENCE OF SUMANGALA. HE DID NOT RECOGNISE HIS DESERTED BRIDE.

WORDS ARE TOO POOR TO DESCRIBE YOUR LOVELINESS!

INDEED, YOU SPEAK PRETTILY!

SUMANGALA ENTERTAINED HIM ROYALLY.

NOW I HAVE YOU IN MY POWER YOU LEARNED FOOL!

YOU DANCE EXCEEDINGLY WELL. AND AS FOR YOUR HOSPITALITY...

LEARNED SIR, DO NOT OUR SCRIPTURES SAY THAT A GUEST IS DIVINITY ITSELF? DO COME AGAIN.

MULADEVA PAID REGULAR VISITS TO SUMANGALA. ONE DAY

MULADEVA, I CAME TO THIS CITY NOT ONLY TO TASTE ITS REFINEMENTS, BUT ALSO TO FIND A SUITABLE HUSBAND. YOU ARE THE MAN I WANT TO MARRY.

THAT WOULD BE MY HEART'S DESIRE.

SUMANGALA AND MULADEVA WERE MARRIED AND HE LIVED AT HER MANSION. AFTER A FEW DAYS

NOW I MUST RETURN TO PATALIPUTRA.

THE NEXT DAY

I HAVE RECEIVED A LETTER FROM MY KING ORDERING ME TO RETURN IMMEDIATELY!

AND WHAT IS YOUR REPLY?

I MUST OBEY MY KING'S COMMAND. BUT WE WILL MEET SOON.

AND SUMANGALA LEFT UJJAINI.

SHE'S GONE — AND I AM BROKEN-HEARTED!

IN DUE COURSE SUMANGALA GAVE BIRTH TO A SON.

THAT DAY, THE BOY CAME HOME QUITE UPSET.

DID YOU FIGHT AGAIN?

MOTHER, WHO IS MY FATHER? AND WHERE IS HE?

LISTEN, SON. I'LL TELL YOU. YOUR FATHER'S NAME IS MULADEVA; HE DESERTED ME AND WENT AWAY TO UJJAINI.

SHE TOLD HIM HER TALE.

I WILL BRING BACK MY FATHER, A CAPTIVE.

SUMANGALA TOLD HER SON HOW TO IDENTIFY MULADEVA AND THE BOY SET OUT FOR UJJAINI.

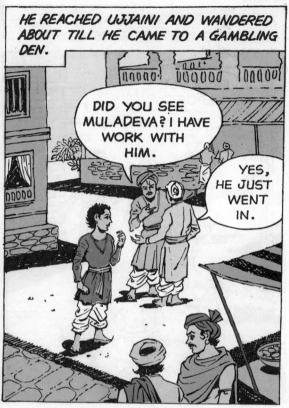

HE REACHED UJJAINI AND WANDERED ABOUT TILL HE CAME TO A GAMBLING DEN.

DID YOU SEE MULADEVA? I HAVE WORK WITH HIM.

YES, HE JUST WENT IN.

ON HEARING MULADEVA'S NAME —

MULADEVA? THAT COULD BE MY FATHER! I'LL FOLLOW THAT MAN.

THE BOY ENTERED THE HALL AND SAW THE MAN HE HAD FOLLOWED SITTING WITH TWO PEOPLE, PLAYING DICE.

I'LL JOIN THEM AND SHOW THEM WHAT MY FINGERS CAN DO AT DICE!

HE JOINED THE OTHERS IN A GAME.

FOR YOUR AGE, YOU PLAY WELL, BOY!

IN NO TIME, THE BOY WON MONEY FROM EVERYONE.

YOU PLAY EXCEEDINGLY WELL! YOU PLAY LIKE A MAN!

THIS IS SMALL SPORT, SIR. I AM ADEPT IN MANY OTHER MATTERS!

THE BOY LEFT, GIVING AWAY THE MONEY TO THE BEGGARS SQUATTING OUTSIDE.

PRINCELY GENEROSITY TOO!

THAT NIGHT WHILE MULADEVA LAY ASLEEP...

...THE BOY ENTERED HIS CHAMBER STEALTHILY.

I MUST GENTLY PLACE HIM ON THE FLOOR AND CARRY OFF THE BEDSTEAD!

HE ARTFULLY PUT MULADEVA ON A HEAP OF SOFT COTTON...

AND MADE OFF WITH THE BEDSTEAD.

HE'LL WAKE UP IN A COMIC SITUATION!

THE NEXT MORNING, MULADEVA AWOKE WITH MIXED FEELINGS OF SHOCK, AMUSEMENT AND SHAME.

SOMEBODY PULLS OFF MY BED FROM UNDERNEATH ME WHILE I REMAIN DEAD ASLEEP...?!

THAT DAY, AS HE WAS PASSING THROUGH THE MARKET SQUARE MULADEVA SAW THE BOY.

THAT IS THE VERY BOY WHO WON AT THE DICE GAME! NOW HE IS SELLING MY BED!

MULADEVA APPROACHED HIM.

WHAT IS THE PRICE OF THIS BEDSTEAD?

I WILL EXCHANGE IT FOR A STRANGE AND WONDERFUL TALE.

WELL, THEN, IF YOU CAN UNDERSTAND MY TALE AND SEE ITS TRUTH, THE BEDSTEAD IS YOURS. IF NOT, I KEEP IT.

THAT'S A BARGAIN!

MULADEVA SPUN HIS TALE.

FAMINE STALKED THE LAND. THE KING COVERED THE BOAR'S BELOVED WITH SHOWERS OF SPRAY FROM CHARIOTS OF SNAKES. WITH THE GRAIN THUS PRODUCED, THE KING PUT AN END TO THE FAMINE.

THE BOY SMILED KNOWINGLY.

THE CHARIOTS OF SNAKES ARE CLOUDS, THE BELOVED OF THE BOAR IS THE EARTH, FOR SHE WAS MOST DEAR TO THE GOD VISHNU IN HIS BOAR INCARNATION; SO ALL YOU ARE SAYING IS THAT THE RAIN FROM THE CLOUDS MADE GRAIN SPRING UP ON THE EARTH!

MULADEVA WAS DUMBFOUNDED AT THE YOUNG BOY'S QUICK GRASP OF FACTS.

NOW HERE'S A STRANGE TALE. IF YOU UNDERSTAND IT AND SEE ITS TRUTH, THE BEDSTEAD IS YOURS. ELSE, YOU SHALL BE MY SERVANT.

I AGREE.

LONG AGO ON THIS EARTH WAS BORN A WONDERFUL BOY. AS SOON AS HE WAS BORN HE MADE THE EARTH TREMBLE WITH HIS WEIGHT. WHEN HE GREW BIGGER HE STEPPED INTO ANOTHER WORLD!

MULADEVA COULD NOT FATHOM THE RIDDLE.

A FALSE STORY, INDEED.

O LEARNED IN THE SCRIPTURES, DID NOT THE GOD VISHNU, WHEN HE TOOK BIRTH AS A DWARF, MAKE THE EARTH TREMBLE, THEN GROW BIGGER AND STEP INTO HEAVEN?

MULADEVA FELT HUMBLED.

SIR, YOU HAVE BEEN DEFEATED BY ME. OWN UP AND BE MY SERVANT, ACCOMPANYING ME WHEREVER I GO.

BOUND BY HIS PROMISE, MULADEVA FOLLOWED HIM AND SOON FOUND HIMSELF IN PATALIPUTRA.

THE BOY LED MULADEVA STRAIGHT TO HIS MOTHER.

WHAT ! SUMANGALA?

YES, BUT ALSO YOUR DESERTED WIFE. TODAY AS I HAD VOWED, YOU HAVE BEEN BROUGHT HERE BY OUR SON.

SUBSCRIBE NOW!

TINKLE COMBO
MAGAZINE + DIGEST
1 year subscription

Pay only ~~₹1200~~ **₹880!**

FREE
2 Time Compass DVDs worth ₹598

TINKLE
MAGAZINE
1 year subscription

Pay only ~~₹480~~ **₹380!**

I would like a one year subscription for
TINKLE COMBO ☐   **TINKLE MAGAZINE** ☐
(Please tick the appropriate box)

YOUR DETAILS*

Name: .... Date of Birth: |__|__| / |__|__| / |__|__|__|__|

Address: ....

.... City: .... Pin: |__|__|__|__|__|__| State: ....

School: .... Class: ....

Tel: .... Mobile: + 91 - |__|__|__|__|__|__|__|__|__|__|

Email: .... Signature: ....

PAYMENT OPTIONS

☐ Cheque /DD:

Please find enclosed Cheque /DD no. |__|__|__|__|__|__|__| drawn in favour of 'ACK Media Direct Pvt. Ltd.'

at .... (bank) for the amount .... ,

dated |__|__| / |__|__| / |__|__|__|__| and send it to: IBH Books & Magazines Distributers Pvt. Ltd., Arch No. 30, West Approach, Below Mahalaxmi Bridge, Mahalaxmi (W), Mumbai - 400034.

☐ Pay Cash on Delivery: Pay cash on delivery of the first issue to the postman. (Additional charge of ₹50 applicable)

☐ Pay by money order: Pay by money order in favour of "ACK Media Direct Pvt. Ltd."

☐ Online subscription: Please visit: www.amarchitrakatha.com

For any queries or further information: Email: customerservice@ack-media.com or Call: 022-40497435 / 36